MATTHEW and TILLY

by REBECCA C. JONES
illustrated by BETH PECK

Dutton Children's Books   New York

Library of Congress Cataloging-in-Publication Data

Jones, Rebecca C.
    Matthew and Tilly/by Rebecca C. Jones; illustrated by Beth
Peck.—1st ed.
        p.   cm.
    Summary: Like all good friends, Matthew and Tilly
have an occasional tiff, but their friendship prevails
despite their differences.
    ISBN 0-525-44684-2
    [1. Friendship—Fiction.]   I. Peck, Beth, ill.   II. Title.
PZ7.J72478Mat   1991   90-3730
[E]—dc20   CIP
                                                      AC

Published in the United States by
Dutton Children's Books,
a division of Penguin Books USA Inc.

Designer: Barbara Powderly

Printed in Hong Kong by South China Printing Co.
First Edition   10 9 8 7 6 5 4 3 2 1

for my brother David,
who always won

R.C.J.

to all the kids
in the neighborhood

B.P.

MATTHEW and TILLY were friends.

They rode bikes together,

and they played hide-and-seek together.

They sold lemonade together. When business was slow,

they played sidewalk games together.

And sometimes they ate ice-cream cones together.

Once they even rescued a lady's kitten
from a tree together.

The lady gave them money
for the bubble-gum machines.

So later they chewed gum together and
remembered how brave they had been.

Sometimes, though, Matthew and Tilly
got sick of each other.

One day when they were coloring,
Matthew broke Tilly's purple crayon. He
didn't mean to, but he did.

"You broke my crayon," Tilly said in
her crabbiest voice.

"It was an old crayon," Matthew said in
his grouchiest voice. "It was ready to break."

"No, it wasn't," Tilly said. "It was a
brand-new crayon, and you broke it. You
always break everything."

"Stop being so picky," Matthew said.
"You're always so picky and stinky and mean."

"Well, you're so stupid," Tilly said.
"You're so stupid and stinky and mean."

Matthew stomped up the stairs.
By himself.

Tilly found a piece of chalk and began drawing numbers and squares on the sidewalk. By herself.

Upstairs, Matthew got out his cash register and some cans so he could play store. He piled the cans extra high, and he put prices on everything. This was the best store he had ever made. Probably because that picky and stinky and mean old Tilly wasn't around to mess it up.

But he didn't have a customer. And playing store wasn't much fun without a customer.

Tilly finished drawing the numbers and squares. She drew them really big, with lots of squiggly lines. This was the best sidewalk game she had ever drawn. Probably because that stupid and stinky and mean old Matthew wasn't around to mess it up.

But she didn't have anyone to play with. And a sidewalk game wasn't much fun without another player.

Matthew looked out the window and wondered what Tilly was doing. Tilly looked up at Matthew's window and wondered what he was doing.

She smiled, just a little. That was enough for Matthew.

"I'm sorry," he called.

"So am I," said Tilly.

And Matthew ran downstairs
so they could play.

Together again.

DATE DUE
